Cornelia Eliza Hood Whipple

A genealogy of Richard Hood:

who came from Lynn, in England, and settled at Lynn, in Massachusetts

Cornelia Eliza Hood Whipple

A genealogy of Richard Hood:
who came from Lynn, in England, and settled at Lynn, in Massachusetts

ISBN/EAN: 9783337373818

Printed in Europe, USA, Canada, Australia, Japan

Cover: Foto ©Raphael Reischuk / pixelio.de

More available books at **www.hansebooks.com**

A GENEALOGY

OF

RICHARD HOOD

.

WHO CAME FROM LYNN, IN ENGLAND, AND
SETTLED AT LYNN, IN MASSACHUSETTS.

BY CORNELIA E. WHIPPLE.

DANVERS:
THE ENDECOTT PRESS,
1899.

PREFACE.

The following Genealogy does not embrace all the families descended from Richard Hood, but only that succession in which the compiler of this work is found.

She is indebted to a little book called "A Genealogy of Richard Hood," by Rev. George Hood and once owned by Richard Hood of Danversport for the record from Richard Hood to Josiah Moulton Hood, her grandfather.

The details—names and dates, intervening—as well as the record of that succession in which the family of the above Richard Hood of Danversport is found can be seen in the little book referred to.

DANVERS, MASSACHUSETTS.
January, 1899.

FAMILY GENEALOGY.

Previous to the year 1650, RICHARD HOOD came from Lynn Regis, Norfolk County, England, and settled on what is now called Nahant, at Lynn, Massachusetts. He owned that peninsular. A house, with a large elm tree before it, now stands on the original site.

Persecution drove him to this country, and tradition says, like many others, he was compelled to forfeit most of his large property.

The settlement of his estate shows him to have been in good circumstances, leaving to each of his *thirteen* children a respectable portion. One brother came with him ; but whether more than one is uncertain. It is possible there were two—John, who settled in Kittery, in Maine, before 1652, and perhaps one in Boston. But this is not probable, inasmuch as the names of Richard and John only are found on the old records.

FIRST GENERATION.

1 **Richard Hood** was born at Lynn Regis, Norfolk County, England, about the year 1630 or 1632, and died at Lynn, Massachusetts, Sept. 12, 1695, aged 63 or 65 years. His wife's name was Mary; but her maiden name, or when or where she was born or married is unknown to the writer. He died first, and his son John settled the estate. Their children were numerous, thirteen in all, of whom NATHANIEL was the fourth.

SECOND GENERATION.

Nathaniel Hood (2), the fourth son of Richard Hood (1) of Lynn Regis, was born about 1672, and was married October 16, 1706 with Joanna Dunnell or Dwinell of Topsfield, Mass. She died Mch. 1, 1732. He died Oct. 30, 1748, aged about 76 years. For a time he lived in Lynn and his elder children were born there; but he removed to Topsfield in 1712, and settled in the extreme northwest part of the town, adjoining Ipswich and Boxford.

Tradition says he with his three older broth-
ers, became a Quaker. This is not uncertain.
His children were not baptized according to
custom ; but none of them were Quakers. His
children numbered 7, of whom JOHN was the
youngest.

THIRD GENERATION.

John Hood (3) of Topsfield, youngest son of
Nathaniel Hood (2), of Lynn, and Joanna
Dwinell, was born Jan. 10, 1724, and was
twice married. His first wife was Elizabeth
Redington. They had four children—three
died in infancy. RICHARD survived. Elizabeth Redington Hood died Oct. 23, 1755.
John Hood served in the war of 1756 and was
with Wolfe on the Plains of Abraham. On
Sept. 14, 1759, he was at the taking of Louis-
burg on Cape Breton Island. He died in Oct.,
1805.

FOURTH GENERATION.

Richard Hood (4) of Topsfield, son of John
Hood (3) and Elizabeth Redington was born

Mch. 1, 1751 and married Lydia Tarbox, Feb. 1775. She was born Sept. 16, 1753 and died Mch. 10, 1824. They lived in Wenham, Mass., and had 5 children, of whom JOSIAH MOULTON was the eldest. There is a stone in the burying ground at Wenham which bears this inscription :

Erected in memory of

MR. RICHARD HOOD,

a soldier of the Revolution

who died Nov. 19, 1835, Aged 84 years.

Also his wife

MRS. LYDIA HOOD,

who died Mch. 10, 1824, aged 70 years.

"They sleep till Death its human prey restore.
When Earth and sky and Time shall be no more."

Richard Hood served in the Revolutionary War eight months in 1775 in Capt. John Baker's Co., Col. Moses Little's Regiment. Also in Capt. Stephen Perkins' Co. which marched on the alarm of April 19, 1775, from Topsfield.

FIFTH GENERATION.

Josiah Moulton Hood (5), eldest son of Rich-

ard Hood (4) and Lydia Tarbox, was born in
Wenham, July 22, 1776, and married Mary
Dodge of Wenham. They lived in Wenham,
and had one child, JOHN. She died in 1806.
Josiah Hood married a second time with Betsey
Cook of Old Hadley, Mass. She was born in
1786 and died Mch. 29, 1852 at Glover, Vt.,
where they had resided. They had two sons:
Calvin H. was born in Sheffield, Vt., Nov. 23,
1823. Philip Perley was born Apr. 12, 1825.
He died at Glover, Vt., Jan. 22, 1844. Calvin
H. Hood is now living at Turner's Falls, Mass.,
1899.

SIXTH GENERATION.

John Hood (6) of Wenham, son of Josiah
Moulton Hood (5) and Mary Dodge, was born
May 8, 1806, and married Rebecca Stanley of
Beverly, Mass., Nov. 29, 1827. She was born
Jan 6, 1808, and died at Danvers, Mch. 22,
1882. He died at Danvers, Oct. 5, 1867.

They resided in Wenham, Danversport and
Danvers. They had nine children:

LYDIA ANN, b. in Wenham, Nov. 20, 1828; d. Oct. 13,
1891.

REBECCA STANLEY, b. Aug. 5, 1830; d. Dec. 26, 1854.

AMANDA BAILEY, b. Wenham, Aug. 19, 1832.

MARY ELIZABETH, b. in Danversport, July 26, 1834; d. Aug. 24, 1895.

WILLIAM HENRY, b. Danversport, Aug. 13, 1836; d. Jan. 15, 1898.

WENDELL PHILLIPS, b. Danversport, Feb. 25, 1839.

JOSEPH EDWARD, b. Danversport, Mch. 26, 1840.

CORNELIA ELIZA, b. Danversport, Mch. 5, 1843.

EMELINE OSGOOD, b. Beverly, now Danvers, July 10, 1845.

SEVENTH GENERATION.

Lydia Ann Hood (7), eldest child of John Hood (6) and Rebecca Stanley, married Charles W. Brown of Wenham, Mass., Dec. 20, 1846. He was born Aug. 25, 1825; died in Danvers, Dec. 1, 1877. They resided a few years in Essex, Mass., afterwards in Danvers.

They had eight children :

FRANCES MARIA, b. Essex, Feb. 26, 1848; d. Essex, Aug. 14, 1849.

MARCIA DODGE, b. Essex, Jan. 15, 1851; d. Danvers, Mch. 18, 1884.

ELLA FRANCIS, b. Essex, June 26, 1854; d. Danvers, 1855.

ELLA AUGUSTA, b. Danvers, Apr. 25, 1856.

CHARLES WALLACE, b. Danvers, Oct. 30, 1859.
LILLIAN FRANCES, b. Danvers, Dec. 26, 1861.
JOSEPH EDWARD, b. Danvers, Oct. 25, 1864.
DENNISON LESLIE, b. Danvers, Feb. 21, 1869.

Rebecca Stanley Hood (7), second child of John Hood (6) and Rebecca Stanley, married Thaddeus Osgood of Danvers, July 14, 1846. He was born in Milford, N. H., Nov. 9, 1827; died in Methuen, Mass., July 9, 1855. They resided in Danvers. They had two children :

> THADDEUS, b. Beverly, now Danvers, Sept. 5, 1847; d. in Beverly, Dec. 9, 1873.
> JOHN HOOD, b. Essex, Apr. 30, 1853; d. Danvers, Jan. 30, 1854.

Amanda Bailey Hood (7), third child of John Hood (6) and Rebecca Stanley, married William B. Jenness of Alton, N. H., May 2, 1851. He was born in Strafford, N. H., July 20, 1828. They have resided in Rochester, Minn., St. Louis, Mo., Casco, Me., Danvers and Alton, N. H. They had five children :

> ALICE AMANDA, b. Casco, Oct. 20, 1854; d. St. Louis, Jan. 29, 1881.
> HARRIETT ELIZABETH, born in Casco, Nov. 10, 1856; d. Albuquerque, N. M., Feb. 28, 1895.

Two infants, (twins) died in Rochester, Minn., and one in Danvers.

Mary Elizabeth Hood (7), fourth child of John Hood (6) and Rebecca Stanley, married Moses Hooper Goodwin of Danvers, Feb. 4, 1856. He was born in Shapleigh, Me., Oct. 27, 1831, and died in Lynn, Mass., May 1, 1880. They resided in Springvale, Me., Danvers and Lynn. They had no children. She married a second time John W. Frost of Springvale, Mch. 11, 1891. He was born in Springvale, Me., May 16, 1827. They resided in Springvale.

William Henry Hood (7), fifth child of John Hood (6) and Rebecca Stanley, married Sarah Lizzie Hammond of Danvers, Sept. 28, 1858. She was born in North Berwick, Me., Jan. 11, 1839; died in Danvers, Oct. 20, 1862. They resided in Danversport, Haverhill and Danvers. They had one child:

> JOSEPH EDWARD, b. Danvers, Aug. 1862; d. Danvers, Sept. 1862.

He married a second time Augusta P. Dodge of New Boston, N. H. She was born Feb. 22, 1834, and died in Danvers, Sept. 28, 1886.

They resided in Danvers and had three children, all b. Danvers :

LIZZIE FRANCES, b. Sept. 9, 1864.
ADDIE REBECCA, b. Feb. 3, 1867.
CALEB BATCHELDER, b. Apr. 14, 1872.

He married a third time Mrs. Clara P. Tufts, of Danvers. She was born in Shapleigh, Me., July 16, 1835, and died in Danvers, Mch. 31, 1894. They resided in Danvers.

Wendell Phillips Hood (7), sixth child of John Hood (6) and Rebecca Stanley, married Maria Phelps Putnam of Danvers, Mch. 27, 1866. She was born in Wenham, Apr. 5, 1843. They resided in Red Wing and Winona, Minn., and in Danvers and Melrose, Mass.

They had three children, all b. Red Wing :

ROBERT PUTNAM, b. Feb. 17, 1868.
WILLIAM PHELPS, b. Apr. 2, 1870; d. in Red Wing,
        Aug. 4, 1870.
SUSAN MABEL, b. May 10, 1876.

Joseph Edward Hood (7), seventh child of John Hood (6) and Rebecca Stanley, married Martha A. Gilpatrick of Danvers, Nov. 13, 1866. She was born in Shapleigh, Me., Mch. 30, 1843, and d. in Danvers, Sept. 6, 1897.

They resided in Danvers.   They had four children, all b. Danvers :

RALPH OTHO, b. July 5, 1870.
CHARLES G., b. Jan. 22, 1873; d. in Danvers, Jan. 22,
  1873.
MABEL, b. June 26, 1877.
LEROY S., b. June 26, 1877; d. in Danvers, May 31,
  1879.

Cornelia Eliza Hood (7), eighth child of John
Hood (6) and Rebecca Stanley, married John
Francis Whipple of Danvers, June 17, 1871.   He
was born in Ipswich, Mass., Aug. 20, 1842.
They have resided in Danvers.   They had two
children, both b. Danvers.

The first, b. Aug. 15, 1873 ; died Aug. 15, 1873.
GUY MONTROSE, b. June 12, 1876.

Emma Osgood Hood (7), ninth child of John
Hood (6) and Rebecca Stanley, resides in Danvers.

EIGHTH GENERATION.

Marcia Dodge Brown (8), daughter of
Charles W. Brown and Lydia Ann Hood (7),
married William S. Inman of Danvers, Apr. 23,

1873. He was born in Tariffville, Conn., May 11, 1847; died in Boston, July 8, 1885. They resided in Danvers and had two children, b. Danvers :

CHARLES THOMAS, b. June 24, 1874.
HATTIE GOODHUE, b. Nov. 27, 1877; d. Danvers, Dec. 31, 1879.

Ella A. Brown (8), daughter of Charles W. Brown and Lydia Ann Hood (7), married Andrew H. Paton of Danvers, June 8, 1875. He was born in Danvers, July 18, 1849. They reside in Danvers, and have had four children, all b. Danvers :

MABEL FLORENCE, Nov. 20, 1876.
MARY IZETTE, b. Aug. 13, 1879.
ANDREW HARRIS, b. Jan. 14, 1882.
LEON BRUCE, b. July 25, 1884.

Charles Wallace Brown (8), son of Charles W. Brown and Lydia Ann Hood (7), married

Ella Josephine Faulkner of Danvers, Dec. 8, 1881. She was born in Andover, Mass., June 26, 1858; died in Salem, Dec. 16, 1893. They resided in Orange Park, Florida, and in Danvers and Salem, Mass. They had one child:

STANLEY FAULKNER, b. Danvers, Mch. 12, 1883.

He married a second time, Mary Ellen Whipple of Salem, Mass., Feb. 28, 1895. She was born in Salem, July 11, 1869. They reside in Salem. Their children are:

HILDA MARION, b. Salem, July 28, 1897.

Lillian F. Brown (8), daughter of Charles W. Brown and Lydia Ann Hood (7), married Herbert Burnham of Peabody, Mass., Sept. 4, 1879. He was born in Manchester, Mass., Apr. 21, 1856. They reside in Stoneham, Mass. Their children are:

MAUD LILLIAN, b. Peabody, May 20, 1880.

HAROLD LEANDER, b. Peabody, July 18, 1882.

Joseph Edward Brown (8), son of Charles W.
Brown and Lydia Ann Hood (7), married Alice
Bolster of Peabody, Mass., Jan. 7, 1891. She
was born in Peabody, Oct. 10, 1867. They reside in Salem.

Dennison L. Brown (8), son of Charles W.
Brown and Lydia Ann Hood (7), married Har-
riet M. Putnam of Danvers, Oct. 11, 1893.
She was born in Danvers, July 13, 1874. They
reside in Salem. Their children are :

MARCIA PUTNAM, b. Salem, June 1, 1895.

Thaddeus Osgood (8), son of Thaddeus Osgood and Rebecca Hood (7), married Anna
Wilson Allen of Beverly, Mass., July 2, 1866.
She was born in Beverly, Sept. 14, 1846. They
resided in Beverly. Their children were:

ELLEN SMITH, b. Beverly, Oct. 12, 1866; d. Beverly,
Sept. 25, 1884.

REBECCA HOOD, b. Beverly, Oct. 7, 1872; d. Beverly,
Jan. 3, 1879.

Alice A. Jenness (8), daughter of William B.
Jenness and Amanda B. Hood, (7) married Nat
Sparhawk of St. Louis, Mo., June 1, 1878. He
was born in St. Louis, in 1850. They resided
in St. Louis. They had one child:

WILLIE JENNESS, b. St. Louis, Feb. 23, 1880.

Lizzie Frances Hood (8), daughter of William H. Hood (7), and Augusta P. Dodge, married Wallace Parker Hood of Danvers, Nov. 10, 1887. He was born in Danversport, Dec. 3, 1863. They reside in Danvers. Their children are :

HELEN DODGE, b. Danvers, Jan. 27, 1892.

Addie Rebecca Hood (8) daughter of William H. Hood (7) and Augusta P. Dodge, married Daniel W. Mason of Pawtucket, R. I., Dec. 16, 1891. He was born in Fall River, Mass., Feb. 8, 1844. They reside in Pawtucket. Their children are :

KENNETH OLIVER, b, Pawtucket, Apr. 12, 1893.

Caleb Batchelder Hood (8), son of William H. Hood (7) and Augusta P. Dodge, married Nina F. Milton of Danvers, Jan. 5, 1898. She was born in Danvers, Jan. 7, 1873. They reside in Danvers Centre, Mass.

Ralph Otho Hood (8), son of Joseph E. Hood (7) and Martha A. Gilpatrick, married Grace B. Hayes of Danvers, Oct. 6, 1898. She was born in Stoneham, Mass., Aug. 21, 1879.

They reside in Baltimore, Md.

Robert Putnam Hood (8), son of Wendell P. Hood (7) and Maria P. Putnam, married Mary A. Campbell of Melrose, Mass., Nov. 3, 1898. She was born in West Bay, Cape Breton, N. S., Aug. 17, 1873. They reside in Melrose.

NINTH GENERATION.

Charles T. Inman, (9), son of William S. Inman and Marcia Dodge Brown (8), married Annie Alber of Danversport, Mass., Apr. 8, 1898. She was born in Danversport, Aug. 1871. They reside in Denver, Colorado.

WAR RECORDS.

FRENCH AND INDIAN WAR.

John Hood, grandson of the first Richard and father of the Revolutionary soldiers hereafter mentioned, served in the "Seven Years' War," generally called the "French and Indian War." He was at the surrender of Cape Breton, July 26, 1758, the first great English success of the war. He was one of the men who scaled the cliffs and stood on the Plains of Abraham when Wolfe, their leader, was killed.--(Authority: Calvin Hood (5), my uncle, now living in Turner's Falls, Mass.)

REVOLUTIONARY WAR.

Richard (3), son of John and Elizabeth Redington Hood, entered the service of his country at the call of the "Lexington Alarm," Apr. 19, 1775, marching from Topsfield, Mass., and enlisting in Capt. Stephen Perkins' Co. Term of service, 2 1-2 days. He enlisted again at Topsfield, May 10, 1775 in Capt. John Baker's Co.,

Col. Little's Regt. Service, 2 m. 27 d.—(Authority : Lexington Alarm Rolls, Vol. 13, p. 68.)

John Hood, born at Topsfield, Feb. 26. 1760, son of John and Mary Kimball Hood, and brother of Richard Hood (3), enlisted in the service at the age of 15. He was at the battle of Bunker Hill, June 17, 1775, on picket duty upon the marsh near by, watching an English vessel to keep her men from landing. Also at the battles of Long Island and White Plains, and crossed the Delaware with Washington on Dec. 8, was in the battle of Princeton and for two months lived, with others, a life of unexampled suffering, without shoes and with clothing of rags going to his home 250 miles distant on foot, begging food on the way.

After a few weeks at home, he re-enlisted ; on Sept. 11, 1777 was in battle of the Brandywine, and on Oct. 4, 1777, in that at Germantown. Went into winter quarters at Valley Forge, Dec. 11, and was discharged in 1778.

In 1779 he went on a privateering cruise, was taken prisoner, carried to Halifax, put on the Prison Ship, where he suffered all but death. He was exchanged and returned to his home.

In Sept, 1780, he was with our troops at the time of Arnold's treachery, and next year at the surrender of Cornwallis.

Thus he was in service 7 of the 8 years of the war.

In 1787, he was again in the field. His native town, Topsfield, was called upon to furnish troops for defence of law and order, at Shay's Rebellion. No one could be found to lead in the enlistment, and failure was imminent. At length a veteran, but 26 years old, enrolled his name, to be followed by others. This veteran was John Hood. The Rebellion was quelled. (Authority : Memorials and Genealogy, by Rev. Geo. Hood, son of above John.)

Samuel Hood, brother of John, born May 1, 1762, was also a Revolutionary soldier. The writer has no record at hand of his service. It was without doubt as brave and faithful as was his brother's.—(Authority : John H. Gould, late of Topsfield, Mass.)

CIVIL WAR.

Wendell Phillips Hood (6), was a student

at Brown University, Providence, R. I., when he heard his country's call to enlist in her defence. He left his studies, and, with many of the young men in the College, was mustered into service, June, 1862, joining Co. A, 10th R. I. Vols., to see service in Virginia. He was discharged at expiration of term of enlistment, Sept., 1862.

He again enlisted Nov. 7, 1862, in Co. F, 48th Mass. Inf. He was acting Hospital Steward at Port Hudson and at Arsenal Hospital, Baton Rouge, La. Also a volunteer nurse on one of the ships of Bank's expedition to the Gulf Dept., where spotted fever was prevalent.

He also saw service at Springfield Landing, near Baton Rouge, where he was sunstruck and had malarial fever from the effects of which he never recovered. He was discharged Sept. 3, 1863.

Joseph E. Hood (6) enlisted July 22, 1862 at Haverhill, Mass., in Co. F, (Capt. S. C. Oliver) 35th Mass. Regt. (Col. Wild.) He was in 21 engagements during his service, notably South Mountain and Antietam, Md., Fredericksburg, Wilderness, Spottsylvania, No. Anna River,

Cold Harbor and Petersburg, Va., Knoxville and Loudon, Tenn., Vicksburg and Jackson, Miss.

He was severely wounded, his left leg being crushed by the explosion of a mine at Petersburg, Va., July 30, 1864, was left to crawl from the enemy's to our lines, whence he was carried to an improvised hospital, where his leg was amputated. This was so carelessly done that a second amputation was necessary, but it was still left in a deplorable state, and he never ceased to suffer from it. He was discharged Apr. 10, 1865, as Sergeant.

William B. Jenness, who married Amanda B. Hood (6), enlisted at Haverhill, Mass., Aug. 1, 1862; was in Co. G, 35th Mass. Regt. He was wounded at the battle of Antietam, Sept. 17, 1862 and discharged Dec. 31, 1862.

John F. Whipple, who married Cornelia E. Hood (6), enlisted in the First Michigan Lancers, (Capt. E. A. Andrews, of Ipswich, Mass.) Nov. 11, 1861. Was transferred to Co. L, 1st Mass. H. A., Feb. 20, 1862, which was stationed south of Washington, establishing de-

fences along the entire line. He was discharged
Feb. 20, 1864 to re-enlist in same Co. and Regt.
two days later. He was wounded in the left
thigh in the battle at Petersburg, Va., June 16,
1864. Was in hospitals at City Point, Va.,
David's Island, N. Y., Readville and Worces-
ter, Mass.

While at the Dale General Hospital, Worces-
ter, he was wounded in the right fore arm by
the premature discharge of a cannon fired in
honor of Lee's surrender. Amputation of hand
was necessary. He was discharged July 3.
1865, for disability.

———

Thaddeus Osgood, son of Thaddeus and Rebecca H (6) Osgood, was mustered into service in the
2d Mass. Unattached Co. Inf. and H. A. (Capt.
Leonard G. Dennis.) He enlisted at Beverly.
This Co. was detailed to the Fort at Gloucester,
and later helped recruit the 23d Mass. Inf.,
that was stationed at Norfolk, Va. He was
discharged at expiration of time of enlistment,
July 7, 1865.

———

William S. Inman, who married Marcia
Dodge Brown (7), was mustered into service

July 15, 1864 : Co. I, 6th Mass. Inf. He was discharged at expiration of service, Oct. 27, 1864. (This Regt. was the "Old Sixth," which went through Baltimore, Apr. 19. 1861, the first of the 9 mos. militia Regts., which were sent forward in 1862, and the first to go forward in 1864.)

ERRATUM.

Instead of the first two lines on page 10, read :

FANNY MAY, b. Rochester, Minn., Mch. 17, 1869; d. Mch. 19, 1869.

WILLINE, b. Rochester, Minn., Mch. 17, 1869; d. July 17, 1869.

www.ingramcontent.com/pod-product-compliance
Lightning Source LLC
Chambersburg PA
CBHW030917260626
47169CB00008B/2882